COSMIC COUSINS

Visit JUPITER

by Andrea Llauget

Illustrations by John McNees

First Edition

PAGE PUBLISHING, INC.
Conneaut Lake, PA

First originally published by Page Publishing 2021

ISBN 978-1-6624-3130-2 (pbk)
ISBN 978-1-6624-3131-9 (digital)

Printed in the United States of America

DEDICATION

This book is dedicated to my family, especially my husband Mike, and my son, Colt. A special thank you to my sister Dawn for your countless hours of help with the creation of this series. Without you it wouldn't have been possible. Thank you to Jake Handler, Author of "Rock on Billy" for your direction and guidance.

Once upon a time, there were four little kid cousins. A girl named Kayla and three boys: Nathan, Jake, and Colt. One of their favorite games was hide-and-seek.

One day Kayla said, "I am tired of only playing around the house, let's play hide-and-seek somewhere else."

Colt replied, "I have an idea. Let's take the rocketship and play hide-and-seek on the eight planets."

Nathan said, "Great idea! We can use the rocketship in our toy room."

Jake raced to the toy room so fast. He yelled, "I go first" because he knew it would make his brother Nathan so mad!

The four little cousins boarded the rocketship. Kayla was the driver because she was the oldest.

Nathan asked, "Which planet do you want to go to first?"

Jake yelled, "Pluto!"

Colt said, "Jake, you are so silly. Pluto isn't a planet. It's a dwarf planet."

Nathan thought about it for a minute and exclaimed, "Let's go to JUPITER because that is the biggest planet."

Kayla yelled, "Buckle up. Off to Jupiter we go!"

The cousins landed on Jupiter, exited the rocketship, and looked around in wonder.

"Who will hide first?" asked Kayla.

Nathan yelled, "Me, I'm always first!"

Colt said, "We will have to count to one hundred because Jupiter is so big."

Kayla, Colt, and Jake covered their eyes and started counting.

Once they reached one hundred, Jake yelled, "Ready or not, here we come!"

E=mc²

The cousins started to look for Nathan, but he was nowhere to be found!

Kayla said, "Where can he be?"

Colt shouted, "I know where he could be. Maybe he is on one of Jupiter's seventy-nine moons."

Jake said, "Seventy-nine MOONS? WHAT!"

Kayla was surprised because she knew Earth only has one moon.

Colt said, "Yes, seventy-nine moons! Isn't that CRAZY?"

Jake said, "It will take forever to search seventy-nine moons. We better get started."

The cousins decided it was safer to stick together to find Nathan on one of Jupiter's seventy-nine moons. As they were looking around, Jake said, "I'm so dizzy. I need to sit down."

Colt interrupted with a fact, "I know why Jake is so dizzy. It's because Jupiter spins so fast that the sun comes up almost every ten hours."

Kayla looked at Colt and replied, "Every ten hours? But on Earth, the sun comes up every twenty-four hours!"

Colt said, "That's right, Kayla."

So Kayla, Cori, and Jake continued to look for Nathan when suddenly Kayla remembered, "Jupiter has a red spot! Maybe Nathan is there."

"Good idea!" shouted Jake. So they raced to the red spot, and guess what they found? Nathan! He was hiding in Jupiter's famous red spot!

Nathan yelled, "Great job guys, you found me!"

Colt's stomach started to grumble. They must have been looking for Nathan on Jupiter for a while because he was getting hungry.

Colt looked at his cousins and said, "Let's go back home and have a snack! I'm hungry." All the cousins agreed; it was time to eat.

The cousins took their seats in the rocketship. Kayla loved being the oldest cousin because she always got to do cool stuff like being the driver.

"Buckle your seat belts!" yelled Colt.

Nathan said, "It was fun being on Jupiter and hiding first."

The four cousins smiled and looked out at all the beautiful stars.

When the cousins landed in their rocketship back in the toy room, Nathan laughed and said, "Race you to the kitchen. I'm first!"
E=mc²

As they were eating, Kayla remembered, "If Jupiter rotates so fast, how long does it take to go around the sun?"

Colt may be younger than Kayla, but he's supersmart.

He said to Kayla, "I read that it takes almost twelve years for Jupiter to go around the sun."

The cousins all looked at each other in amazement because they knew that it takes Earth only one year to go around the sun.

Before taking another bite of his peanut butter and jelly sandwich, Nathan said, "Let's go to a different planet tomorrow and play a different game."

All of the cousins nodded in agreement and ate their snack.

It was a great day on Jupiter!
E=mc²

QUIZ TIME

How well do you know the solar system?

1. How many moons does Jupiter have?
2. Is Pluto one of the eight planets?
3. What is the biggest planet in the solar system?
4. How long does it take for Jupiter to go around the sun?
5. How long does it take Earth to go around the sun?

See answers below.

1. Seventy-nine.
2. No, it's a dwarf planet.
3. Jupiter.
4. About twelve Earth years.
5. One year (365 1/4 days).

ABOUT THE AUTHOR

Andrea Mondadori Llauget was raised in Rutherford, New Jersey, with her two younger sisters, Dawn and Leah, by their parents, Doreen and Steve Mondadori. Andrea always had a passion for educating and has been teaching business at West Essex High School in North Caldwell, NJ since 2001. She loves being active in her community as the head softball coach and student council advisor. Andrea was her school's recipient of the NJ Governor's Educator of the Year for the 2020–2021 school year.

Andrea currently serves on the advisory board for Angelwish.org. Andrea is married to her husband, Mike. They have a son named Colt and two dogs, Cosmo Kramer and Cal Ripken III. Colt loves nothing more than playing with his cousins Kayla, Nathan, Jake, Natalia, and Brooklyn. Andrea and her family currently reside in Fairfield, New Jersey.

Instagram: @cosmiccousinsbooks
Website: www.cosmiccousinsbooks.com

CPSIA information can be obtained
at www.ICGtesting.com
Printed in the USA
BVHW020222290321
603627BV00021B/1334